Here's Monster Dot.
Does she have spots?
Yes, lots and lots and lots and lots.

But her friend Ugg, he has none—
not twenty, not ten, not even one.

Zero spots is just no fun.

Here's Monster Spike.
Does he have spots?
Yes, lots and lots and lots and lots.

But Monster Ugg, he still has none—
not thirty, not seven, not even one.
Zero spots is just no fun!

Here's Monster Sue.
Does she have spots?
Yes, lots and lots and lots and lots.

But Monster Ugg, he still has none—
not a hundred, not two, not even one.
Zero spots is just no fun!

After a while, Ugg started to cry.
"I wish I had spots," he said with a sigh.

"Don't be sad," said Monster Sue.
"From head to toe, you're special, too."

"Just look in the mirror—
you're brilliant blue!"

"Blue like the ocean, blue like the sky, blue like a blue jay and blueberry pie!"

Ugg had to admit, Sue's words were right.
His spotlessness WAS quite a sight!

From that day on, Ugg loved his skin
and never wanted spots again.
Yes, lots of spots do add some spice,
but zero spots sure does look nice.

**Can you find...**

a monster, a snake, and a cow with zero spots, not to mention a dragon, a dog, and a pair of robots?

What other creatures with zero spots do you see?

# 0 Cheer

## Hooray for Zero!

Let's clap and tap
and touch the ground.
Let's jump and thump
and spin around.
Let's wave and wiggle
and cheer and shout
for a wonderful number
we can't live without:
ZERO!